HOUGHTON MIFFLIN COMPANY BOSTON

The Riverside Press Cambridge

1951

Wicked John and the Devil

TOLD BY
Richard Chase
PICTURES BY
Joshua Tolford

To the boys + girls
of Evanston,
with good wishes of
Richard Cha[se]

Feb. 1952

Based on an oral version I first heard
told by Mrs. Jenning L. Yowell of Al-
bemarle County, Virginia.

Richard Chase

I

One time there was an old blacksmith named John.
I don't know where he lived at, but when I was a
boy and heard the old folks tell the tale I always thought
it all happened somewhere here in the mountains.

Anyhow, Old John he was so mean they called him
Wicked John. Mean? A-a Law! He was a rough
'un! Independent minded, didn't care about nothin'
nor nobody. Talked mean, acted mean. Never did
go to church-meetin'. And he even worked of a Sunday.

One thing about him, though: he always did treat a stranger right. Everwhen a stranger come through there, everybody in the settle-ment would treat him sus-picious-like, talk about him behind his back 'n all — everybody but Old John. So one mornin' Wicked John was workin' there in his shop when an old beg-gar came to the door: crippled-up, walkin' on two sticks, all bent over with rheumatism, looked right tired and hungry-like. Stood there lookin' in, and fin'lly Old John hollered at him, says:

"Come on in! Come inside and rest a while, if you ain't in no hurry."

2

The old beggar he heaved over the doorsill, sat there on the big sill-beam, and Old John tried to talk to him. Seemed like the old man was just about give out. John he fin'lly laid his hammer down and went to the house. Came back with a big plate full of vittles: boiled sweet potato, big chunk of ham-meat, greens, beans, a slice of cake, and a tall glass of sweet-milk.

"Here, old man! Try these rations. I hope you can find somethin' here you can eat."

"Thank ye. Thank ye, kindly."

"O hit ain't much, but you're welcome, you're welcome."

Wicked John went on back to work a-hammerin'
and a-poundin' there at his anvil, and the beggar-man
started eatin'.   Old John he was watchin' him out one
corner of his eye; and pretty soon he saw the old beg-
gar lay the plate and glass to one side and start to
get up.

He let them two sticks fall to the ground when he
raised up, and then he commenced straightenin' up,
straightenin' up, and all the kinks came out of him,
and the next thing Wicked John knew——there, r'ared
up in the door, was a big stout-like man with a long
white beard and white hair, white robe right down to
his feet, and he had a big key in his hand.

Old John had done dropped his hammer and was a-
standin' there with his jaw hangin' down and his eyes
popped open.

4

Says, "Con-found!"

"John, I don't reckon you know me, do ye?"

"Well now! Why, what happened to that old beggar? And where-in-the-nation do you come from where folks dress like that?"

"I don't reckon you got any way of knowin' me, John, since you never have been to Sunday school or church since the day you were born. — I'm Saint Peter."

Wicked John r'ared back and laughed. Says, "Aw, now! You expect me to believe that?"

"That don't differ. I'll just tell you how-come I'm here. Once a year I come down and walk the earth to see can I find any decent folks left on it. And the first man I run across that treats me right, I always give him three wishes. So you go ahead now, John, and wish three times. Just wish for anything you've

6

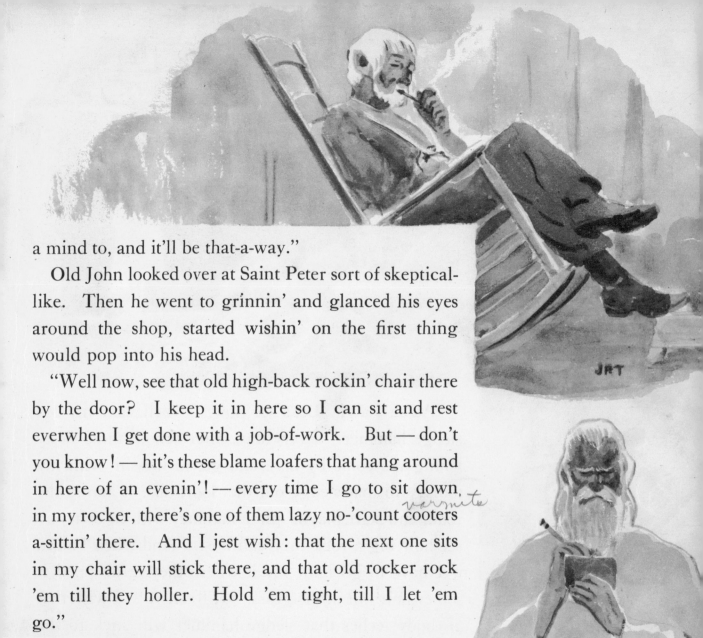

a mind to, and it'll be that-a-way."

Old John looked over at Saint Peter sort of skeptical-like. Then he went to grinnin' and glanced his eyes around the shop, started wishin' on the first thing would pop into his head.

"Well now, see that old high-back rockin' chair there by the door? I keep it in here so I can sit and rest everwhen I get done with a job-of-work. But — don't you know! — hit's these blame loafers that hang around in here of an evenin'! — every time I go to sit down, in my rocker, there's one of them lazy no-'count cooters a-sittin' there. And I jest wish: that the next one sits in my chair will stick there, and that old rocker rock 'em till they holler. Hold 'em tight, till I let 'em go."

Saint Peter was writin' it down in a little gold note-book. Says, "That's one, John."

"Aa-aa Law! Let's see now. — Well, take my old sledge hammer. Every day, after school these fiesty young'uns come by here and get to messin' with my tools: slip that sledge out the door, take it across the road, and start playin' pitch-hammer with it, or try to see how big a rock they can bust. And when I need it I have to go hunt for it where they've dropped it somewhere out in the grass. — I'll tell ye! I wish that *any*body teches that sledge hammer will stick to the handle, and hit pound right on, shake 'em — shake the daylights out of 'em — till I let 'em go."

8

Well, Saint Peter he was lookin' kind of sorry, like he thought Old John was wastin' his wishes pretty bad; but John was mean, like I said. *He* didn't care! Looked at Saint Peter right mischievous-like, grinned again, says:

"One more wish, huh, Peter? — All right. Now: There's my big firebush just outside the door, one of them old-time thornbushes, gets full of red blossoms real early in the spring of the year. I like my old firebush, but hit's been mommicked up right bad here lately: folks backin' their wagons over it, horses trom-

9

plin' on it; and these hifalutin' folks comin' over the mountain a-fox-huntin' — Ha! — gallopin' all around in my pasture field in their little red coats. Looks like they got to stop and break ridin' switches off my fire-brush every time they pass here. — I wish that old bush would grab the very next one teches it: grab 'em and pull 'em right down in the middle where them stickers are the thickest, and hold 'em there — till I let 'em out."

Saint Peter quit writin' and shut that little book,

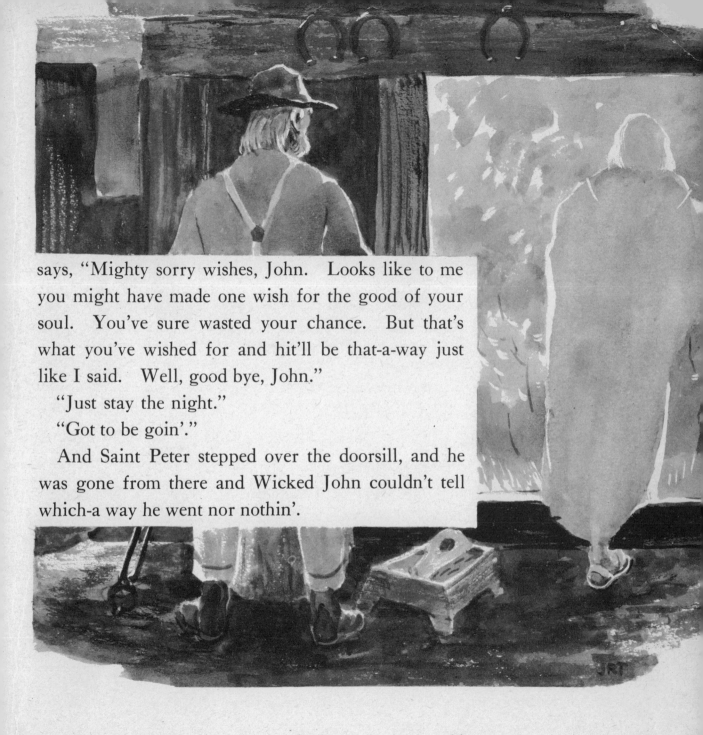

says, "Mighty sorry wishes, John.   Looks like to me you might have made one wish for the good of your soul.   You've sure wasted your chance.   But that's what you've wished for and hit'll be that-a-way just like I said.   Well, good bye, John."

"Just stay the night."

"Got to be goin'."

And Saint Peter stepped over the doorsill, and he was gone from there and Wicked John couldn't tell which-a way he went nor nothin'.

II

Well, after that Old John got to actin' meaner than ever. He caught a lot of folks in his chair and on that hammer handle, and every time anybody happened to brush against that firebush it would grab 'em and they'd get scratched up right pityful. So it wasn't long till Wicked John turned so contrary and biggity that he was the meanest man in the world. And one day the Devil he heard about it, and he decided that wouldn't do: havin' anybody beat *him* in meanness. So he sent for Wicked John, sent one of his little devils to fetch him right then.

So Old John looked up one day and there, standin'
in the door, was a little horn-ed devil.

"Come on, old man. Daddy sent me to get ye.
Said for me to take ye, and come right on back."

Old John had his hammer raised up, lookin' at
that little devil; started in hammerin' again, says, "All
right, son. I'll be ready to go with ye in just a few
more licks. Reckon you'll let me finish this one last
horseshoe. Come on in. I'll not be but a minute or
two."

"No.   Daddy said not to wait."

"All right.   I'll be as quick as I can.   Come on in."

Well, the little devil stepped over in the shop, watched Wicked John hit a few licks, and then he saw that old rockin' chair.   He made for it, eased down in it, r'ared back and started rockin'.   Says:

"You hurry up then.   Daddy'll be mad if I take too long."

Wicked John finished that horseshoe, soused it in the coolin' tub, threw it on the ground, and then he reached with his tongs and picked up another'n.

"Hey, old man! You said jest one!" — And that little devil tried to get up but the more he tried the worse that old chair rocked him, his head a-goin' *wham! bang!* against the chairback, and he went to hollerin' and beggin' Wicked John to turn him loose.

"I'll let you go if you get on out of here and promise not to bother me no more."

"Yes sir! I'll leave right now, and I'll not *never* come back."

"All right. Away with ye!"

And the rockin' chair throwed him out in the floor, and when he got his legs under him — *whippity-cut!* — out the door he flew.

A few minutes after that first devil was gone here
came another one, a little bigger'n the first 'un.   Stood
there in the door actin' biggity.   Says:

"You come on here, old man."

"Why hello, son.   Come on in."

Old John went right on workin'

"You stop that poundin' now, and come with me."

"Why, I can't stop now.   Got this thing red hot
and I'm bound to finish it, 'fore we go."

"No, sir.   You got to quit and come on right now.

Ye hear?   Daddy said if I didn't bring you back in three minutes he'd scorch me good."

Wicked John was a-poundin' right on.

"Huh?   Can't hear ye.   I can't talk till I get done with this wagon tire.   I just now took it out the forge."

The little devil saw how Old John was havin' it kind of awkward the way he had to hold that big iron wagon tire up with one hand and try to beat it with the other.

18

So he lumbered right on inside the shop, says:

"Stand back then, old man. You hold that thing up and let me pound it. We got to hurry."

Leaned over and picked up the big sledge hammer and started swingin' it. Wicked John he held the tire up and turned it where it had to be worked, and when it was done, he pulled it out from under the hammer, cooled it and leaned it against the wall.

"Much obliged. — Hit's finished What ye pound-in' so hard for?" says Old John and went to laughin'.

Well, the way that hammer was a-swingin' that little devil around and around, and a-jerkin' him up and down with his legs a-flyin' ever' which-a-way — hit was a sight in this world!

"Ow! My hands is stuck!—O please, mister!
Please make this thing turn me loose!"

"You promise to leave?"

"Shore, I promise!"

"And not come back?"

"Yes sir! No sir! You won't never catch *me* here
again."

"Then away with ye!"

So the hammer turned him loose. Flung him up
in the rafters! And when he landed and got his legs
untangled, out the door he streaked.

21

Then it wasn't hardly no time till Wicked John looked up, and there standin' in the door, with his old goat horns roached back over his head and his old tail just a-switchin' and that big cow's foot of his'n propped up on the sill, was the Old Boy himself. Stood there just a-glowerin'.

Old John let him stand, just kept right on with his work. Says:

"Howdy do! Come on in."

"YOU COME ON NOW, OLD MAN. AND I AIN'T GOIN' TO TAKE NO FOOLISHNESS OFF YE NEITHER!"

"All right, sir. Just as soon as I get done sharpenin' this mattick. Hit won't take more'n another lick or two. Come on in and sit down."

"NO! I'LL NOT SIT IN NO CHAIR OF YOUR'N!"

"Suit yourself. But now, we'll be ready to go quicker'n you can say 'Scat!' if you'll just give this mattick head a couple of licks while I hold it here.

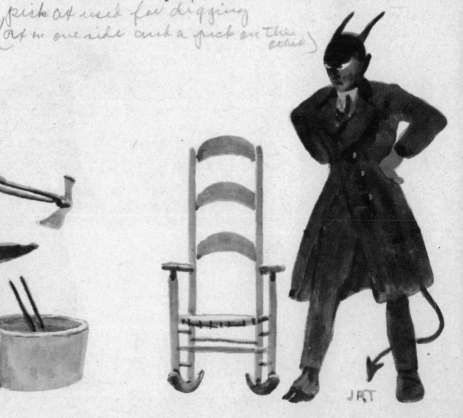

You can take the big sledge leanin' there on the door-sill, and . . . ."

"NO!   I AIN'T GOIN' TO TECH NO SLEDGE NEITHER.   YOU DONE MADE ME MAD ENOUGH ALREADY, OLD MAN.   I DIDN'T LIKE IT A BIT THE WAY YOU DONE MY BOYS, AND I'M A-TAKIN' YOU OFF FROM HERE RIGHT NOW.   YOU HEARD ME!"

And the old Devil made a grab for Wicked John. Old John backed off, says:

"You and who else? You just tech me. I dare ye!"

The Devil nabbed him by the collar, and then John let him have it: punchin' and kickin' and buttin'. They had several rounds there by the door and the old Devil was gettin' madder and madder. Fin'lly he caught him a hold on the seat of Old John's britches and heaved him out the door, says:

"BLAST YE, OLD MAN! I'M GOIN' TO LICK THE HIDE OFF YOU RIGHT NOW. YOU'LL SEE!—WHERE'LL I GET ME A SWITCH?"

He looked around, saw that firebush, and reached to break him off a switch. And time he touched it the bush grabbed him and wropped all around him, jerked him headforemost right down in the middle of all them long stickers. The old Devil he tried to squirm out but the more he thrashed around in there the worse scratched up he got, till fin'lly he gave up, with his old legs a-hangin' limp out the branches.

27

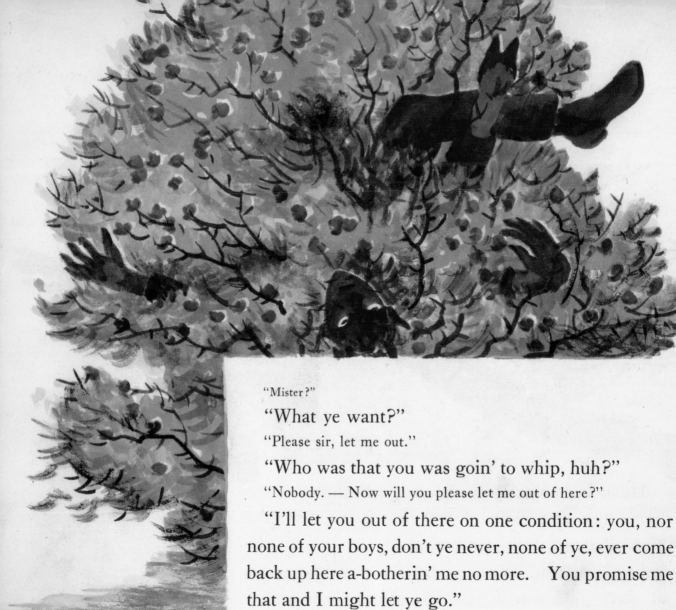

"Mister?"

"What ye want?"

"Please sir, let me out."

"Who was that you was goin' to whip, huh?"

"Nobody. — Now will you please let me out of here?"

"I'll let you out of there on one condition: you, nor none of your boys, don't ye never, none of ye, ever come back up here a-botherin' me no more.   You promise me that and I might let ye go."

"I promise.   Now, will you please make this bush turn loose of me?"

28

"Away with ye then!"

So the bush let go, and when the Devil came out of it he had leaves stuck on his horns and trash all over him. And such a kickin' up dust you never did see! They tell me that when the Old Boy left there he wasn't moseyin'.

III

So Wicked John never was bothered by any devils after that, and he just kept right on blacksmithin' there in his blacksmith shop. He stayed mean, too, just as mean as ever — right to the day he died. And when, fin'lly, he did die, he didn't do a thing but go right straight up to The Pearly Gates. Knocked — *Bam! Bam!* — and Saint Peter opened up a little crack, looked out, says:

"*Uh*-oh! — Well, John, what ye want?"

"Why-er — Peter, seein' as you knowed me, I sort of thought that maybe . . ."

"Why, John! You can't come in here."

"Oh, I know I can't stay. Just let me in to take a look around, and then I'll go."

"Can't do it, John. You wait a minute. — I reckon I'll have to show ye your accounts in the record book."

Saint Peter reached just inside the door and got out a big book, says:

"Here's your pages in the ledger, John. You can see for yourself. — Now, here's your credit side, and it's plumb blank. Just two or three entries 'way up at the top of the page. But over here on the *other* side — Why! — Hit's full clean down to the bottom, and all the meanness you've done in the past seven years had to be writ in sideways."

Saint Peter folded the book up, says:

"I'm sorry but I can't let you put even one foot inside here. So if you'll excuse me now . . ."

And Saint Peter went back in and started shuttin' the gates to.

Well, Old John he turned around, and down the stairsteps he started—— down, down, down.

IV

That day it happened there were three or four little devils playin' — playin' catch with a ball of fire — there in front of the Gate to Hell, and one of 'em was that first 'un was sent to fetch Wicked John. He chanced to look off down the road directly — and

then he ran through the gates just a-squallin':

"Daddy! O daddy! Run here quick!"

The old Devil came and looked out. And there, with his hands in his pockets a-whistlin' and just a-weavin' up the road, was Wicked John.

The Devil turned around, says:

"Bar the door, boys!   Shut them gates, quick now."

The little devils grabbed the big gates and slammed 'em to in a hurry, and the Devil clamped a big pad-

lock on.   So when Wicked John got there and looked
through the bars there stood the old Devil, 'way back,
with his young'uns a-peekin' out from behind his coat-
tails just a-tremblin'.

And time **Old John** looked inside, the Devil hollored at him, says:

"Un-*unh*! You ain't comin' in *here* now! I done had enough of ye! You turn around and put off."

Old John stood there scratchin' his head, says:

"Con-found! Now what-in-the-nation am I goin to do? Saint Peter just told me I couldn't get in up there, and here *you* done locked me out. Why, I don't know where to go to now."

The Devil he studied a minute, then he grabbed up some tongs and reached in the furnace and got hold of a hot coal. He edged over one side of the gate and handed the tong-handles out the bars, says:

"Here, old man, you just take this chunk of fire, and go on off somewhere else, and start you a hell of your own."

Old John took it, and put off.

And they tell me that, right to this day, down in the Great Dismal Swamp, somewhere down yonder between Virginia and Carolina, you can look out of a night and see a little bob of light movin' around out there.

One old-time name for it is the will-o'-the-wisp, but my grandaddy always called it the Jacky-my-lantern. Of course, these here folks that don't know no better — these schoolteachers and college professors — they'll try to tell ye that it ain't nothin' but marsh gas a-lightin' up out there in the swamp.

But I reckon you-all know, now, who it is.